★ TODAY'S ★
HEROES

Joni Eareckson Tada

D0068483

Other Books in the Today's Heroes Series

Ben Carson
Colin Powell
David Robinson

★ TODAY'S ★
HEROES

Joni Eareckson Tada

Gregg & Deborah Shaw Lewis

Zonderkidz

Today's Heroes: Joni Eareckson Tada
Copyright © 2002 by Gregg and Deborah Shaw Lewis

Requests for information should be addressed to:

Zonder**kidz**™

The children's group of Zondervan
Grand Rapids, Michigan 49530
www.zonderkidz.com

ISBN: 0-310-70300-X

Photography © Ken Taylor
Cover Design: Lookout Design Group
Interior design by Todd Sprague

Printed in the United States of America

02 03 04 05 06 07 / DC/ 10 9 8 7 6 5 4 3 2 1

CONTENTS

1

THE ACCIDENT

The calm, cool, inviting water took on the red glow of the setting sun at the end of another hot July day. Sixteen-year-old Joni Eareckson swam alone out into Chesapeake Bay, away from her older sister, Kathy, and the friends she had come with, to a small wooden raft where she pulled herself out of the water.

As she stood and shook herself off, Joni's new blue swimsuit shone almost purple in the reflected evening light. *What a great time and place to swim!* she thought as she stood, balancing herself with her toes curled over the edge of the raft. She slowly raised her arms over her head, flexed her knees, and made an easy, graceful dive into the murky bay.

As she broke the surface the cool water closed around her body—the last thing Joni's arms and legs would ever feel. Then everything seemed to happen at once, but in a watery slow-motion blur.

Joni felt her head strike something hard. Her arms and legs sprawled awkwardly out of control. She heard a strange buzz. A vibration pulsed through her body—like a small electrical shock.

The next thing she knew, Joni was drifting face down underwater wondering, *How did I get here? Why are my arms tied to my chest? I must be caught in a fishnet or something.* She struggled with all her might to break free. Nothing happened. *My legs are caught too.*

A gentle tidal swell lifted and rolled her along the bottom. Joni felt the pressure of holding her breath begin to build. Trying to move, she felt like she was in a dream. But she knew she wasn't asleep. Panic seized her. *What's happening? If I don't breathe, I'm gonna drown. And I don't want to die! Somebody, help me! Please!*

Another swell lifted her off the bottom just a few inches. As she settled back down again, she wondered if this was what it felt like to die. Bits of images, familiar faces, and partial thoughts flashed through her mind. Friends. Sisters. Her parents. Scenes from childhood. Things she was ashamed of. So many memories . . .

2

IN THE
EMERGENCY ROOM

Joni practically grew up outdoors. From the time she could toddle around her family's Maryland farm, Joni wandered and explored the nearby fields and forests. And she absolutely loved horses.

Once she got big enough to ride her own pony, she just *had* to keep up with her older sisters on their big horses. But since her little pony was only half the size of her sisters' mounts, she had to gallop twice as fast.

Joni enjoyed the challenge of that until they came to the edge of a river. Her sisters always looked for the deepest place to splash across on their big horses. They never seemed to notice that Joni and her pony were so much smaller and sank a lot deeper into the rushing waters. That scared Joni, but she wasn't about to let her sisters know it.

She never forgot one time at the Gorsuch Switch Crossing on the Patapsco River. Rain earlier in the week had swelled the river to the top of its banks. Her sisters plunged in and waded their horses toward midstream. Joni paused only a moment before she started her pony across. But she stared at the water swirling and churning around the shaking legs of her pony until she felt dizzy and began to lose her balance in the saddle.

Her sister Jay called back to her, "Look up, Joni! Keep looking up!" And sure enough, as soon as she took her eyes off the water and focused on her sisters, she regained her balance and made it the rest of the way across.

Many of Joni's happiest memories involved her sisters . . . like the time she and Kathy lugged wood, collected nails, and then borrowed a couple of hammers to construct a sturdy tree house just far enough from their farmhouse that it seemed like a private hideaway far from adults. It wasn't just a shelter or a place to hide but protection from the rain beating on the tin roof and the wind shaking the branches of the tree. It made Joni feel safe.

Most of her family memories made her feel that way because the Eareckson family was a close and loving one headed by her father, Johnny (whom she was named after), and her mom, Lindy. Jay, Kathy, and Linda were her sisters.

The Earecksons enjoyed doing all sorts of things together—from traveling and camping out

West, to trail rides and backpacking, and regularly attending church.

Joni had always been healthy and athletic. Being named captain of her high school lacrosse team had been just as important to her as her good grades and nomination to the National Honor Society. And now that she had graduated from high school just weeks before, she planned to go away from home to college that coming fall.

So many things flashed through Joni's mind as she drifted helplessly along the bottom of Chesapeake Bay that beautiful July evening in 1967. She still couldn't move. She wanted to scream, "Help! Somebody help me!" But when the next tidal swell lifted her a little higher, she just as quickly dropped back to the bottom where broken shells, stones, and sand scraped against her shoulders and face.

"Joni!" A muffled voice filtered down through the water from above.

Joni could hear her sister wading nearer. *Help me, Kathy! I'm stuck!*

"Joni! Are you looking for shells?"

No. I'm caught down here! Grab me! I can't hold my breath much longer!

"Did you dive in here, Joni? It's so shallow."

Joni could hear her sister clearly now. She felt Kathy's arms around her shoulders trying to lift her. She had no more air. Everything began to go dark. Kathy stumbled and let go. Then she lifted Joni again.

Just before she fainted, Joni's head came out of the water. She choked and gagged and gulped in mouthfuls of air.

"Thank you! Thank you, God!" she gasped.

"Are you okay?" Kathy wanted to know.

Joni wasn't okay. She was scared. Confused. Her arm still felt as if it were tied to her chest, but she could see it now draped over Kathy's shoulder. She looked down and realized all her limbs were just dangling there in the water. She couldn't move them. *Why?*

Kathy took charge. She called to a nearby swimmer with an inflatable raft. Together they wrestled Joni into it and pushed her toward shore. When she heard the raft scrape on the sand beneath her, Joni tried to get up. But she felt pinned to the raft.

A crowd of swimmers quickly gathered and hovered over and around her. Their whispers and stares embarrassed Joni. "Make them leave, Kathy," she begged.

"Everyone stand back," her sister ordered. "Give her room. And someone call an ambulance."

Joni could see the concern on her sister's face. "Kathy—I can't move. Hold me!"

"I am, Joni!" She held up Joni's hands to show her.

"But I can't feel it! Squeeze me!" Joni said.

Kathy leaned over and held her sister close. Then she touched Joni's leg. "Can you feel this?"

"No," Joni replied.

"This?" Kathy squeezed Joni's forearm.

"No!" Joni cried. "I can't feel it."

"How about this?" Her hand slid from Joni's arm to rest on her shoulder.

"Yes! Yes!" Joni exclaimed. "I can feel that!" Relief swept over her. She could feel something. She lay in the raft trying to make sense of it all. *I hit my head diving. I must have injured something that caused this numbness. How long is it gonna last?*

"Don't worry," she told her sister. "The Lord won't let anything happen to me. I'll be all right."

Soon Joni heard the wail of a siren drawing closer. An ambulance pulled up and its doors opened. In a matter of minutes the paramedics carefully lifted her onto a stretcher, loaded her into the back of the ambulance, and belted her down. Kathy climbed in alongside her injured sister. The siren wailed again as they pulled away from the beach.

"I hate to put you to all this trouble," Joni told the ambulance attendant leaning over her. "Once I catch my breath I think I'll be okay. I'm sure the numbness will wear off soon."

He didn't say anything. He just reached over and gently brushed the sand off her face, smiled, and then looked away. Joni wished he'd tell her everything would be all right. But he didn't say a word.

By the time the ambulance pulled into the hospital emergency entrance, the sun had set. It was dark outside. Joni felt very cold. And she wanted nothing more than to go home.

Inside, the emergency room bustled with activity. Joni was taken through some swinging doors and transferred onto a hospital table with wheels. The bright overhead lights hurt her eyes. All the equipment—the scissors, the scalpels, the tubes, the machines—frightened her. The antiseptic hospital smell made her feel sick to her stomach.

A nurse strapped Joni to the table, rolled her into an examination cubicle, and pulled the privacy curtains closed. Joni tried again to move her arms and legs. Nothing happened. She felt helpless and scared. Tears began trickling down her cheeks. But she couldn't brush them away.

"Can't you tell me what's happening to me?" she begged the nurse.

The woman just shrugged and began taking off Joni's rings. "The doctor will be here soon. I'm going to put your jewelry in this envelope. Hospital regulations."

"How long will I have to stay here?" Joni asked. "Will I be able to go home tonight?"

"I'm sorry. You'll have to ask the doctor. Regulations." Her emotionless response reminded Joni of a telephone recording. The nurse placed the envelope of jewelry on a nearby table, opened a drawer, and pulled out a large pair of shears. She walked back toward Joni with the scissors in her hand.

"Wh-what are you going to do?" Joni asked her.

"I've got remove your swimming suit."

"You can't cut it. I just got it. It's my fav—"

"Sorry. Regulations," the nurse repeated. The heavy ch-cluk, ch-cluk, ch-cluk of the scissors seemed to echo through the ER. When the woman pulled the ruined scraps of material off and dropped them in a nearby waste can, Joni wanted to scream at her. But all she did was cry.

The nurse did pull a sheet over Joni before she left. But Joni felt embarrassed and uncomfortable. And when the sheet slipped partway off, she couldn't even reach down and cover herself. Frustration and fear brought more tears.

Joni whispered parts of the Twenty-third Psalm and tried to keep her mind off where she was and what was happening. She thought about her mom and dad and her boyfriend. *Has anyone told them yet? Where are they?*

A man in a white lab coat pulled the curtain aside and stepped into the cubicle. "I'm Dr. Sherrill," he said as he flipped through the pages on his clipboard. "And your name is . . . Joanie?"

"It's pronounced Johnny," she told him. "I'm named after my father."

"Okay, Joni. Let's see what happened to you."

"Dr. Sherrill, when can I go home?"

He didn't answer. "Tell me, do you feel this?" He had a long pin and was pricking her feet and legs.

"No. I can't feel that." She wished someone would tell her what that meant.

"How about this?"

Joni gritted her teeth and shut her eyes to concentrate, hoping to feel something. Anything. "No, nothing."

The doctor gently took Joni's arm and pressed the pin against her fingers. Her hand. Her wrist. Her forearm. *Why can't I feel anything?* she wondered. He touched her upper arm. Finally she felt a prickling in her shoulder.

"I feel that," she told the doctor. "I had feeling there at the beach too."

Dr. Sherrill took out a pen and began to write on the clipboard.

Other medical staff appeared. Dr. Sherrill went through the pin routine again as a second doctor watched. "Looks like a fracture-dislocation," the two of them agreed. Joni had no idea what that meant. But when they talked about ordering the operating room prepped, she understood what they were planning.

"And try again to reach her parents."

That meant her parents didn't know she was there. Joni felt more scared and alone than ever.

Someone wiped her arm with a cotton ball and stuck a needle in a vein. She didn't feel that either. But out of the corner of her eye, she saw Dr. Sherrill holding a pair of electric hair clippers. She heard a loud click and the clippers began to buzz.

"No!" she cried. "Please! Not my hair!" She began to sob as the clippers slid across her scalp, and she saw chunks of damp blonde hair fall to the table and onto the floor. A nurse prepared a soapy lather, picked up a razor, and walked toward Joni.

The room began to spin and then go dim. Joni's stomach churned.

Then she heard a high-pitched noise—a cross between a buzz and a squeal. She turned her head to look. *It's a drill!* She felt someone turn and hold her head as the drill began grinding into the side of her skull.

Finally, the anesthesia kicked in and Joni began to feel drowsy. She tried to fight it. *What if I don't wake up? Will I ever see my family and friends again? Oh, God, I'm afraid.*

She saw faces. She heard voices. But nothing made sense. The room grew dark and the noise faded. For the first time since the dive, she felt relaxed—even peaceful. It no longer mattered that she was paralyzed, lying on a table with her head shaved. The drill no longer threatened her as she drifted into a deep, deep sleep.

3

PERMANENT PARALYSIS

Coming out of the darkness, Joni thought she heard the drill. She tried to wake up enough to scream, "Stop!" She didn't want them drilling into her head while she was awake. But no words sounded.

She forced her eyes open. But the room was spinning.

There was no drill—just the steady hum of an air conditioner.

As her head cleared, Joni tried to remember where she was. She looked up at the ventilator grill above her head. Beyond that she saw a cracked plaster ceiling. *I'm still in the hospital.* When she tried to move her head to see the rest of the room, sharp pain bit into the side of her head. She realized the pain had something to do with the holes they had drilled in the sides of her head. And out of the corner of her eyes she could see large metal tongs attached to a spring-like contraption that held her head firmly in place.

Joni lost consciousness again and drifted in and out for days. She didn't know when she was asleep or when she was awake because the pain, the drugs the doctors prescribed, and the disorienting surroundings combined to turn everything into one big nightmare. She thought she was losing her mind.

When someone's loud moaning finally awakened her again, Joni found herself lying face down. The tongs were still clamped into her head, and her body was suspended in some kind of canvas frame. There was an opening in the canvas for her face. But lying face down, all she could see was a small section of the tile floor beneath her. A pair of legs with white shoes and nylon hose stood at the edge of her field of vision.

"Nurse!" she called out.

"Yes. I'm right here."

"Where . . . er . . . what . . . uh . . ." Joni stammered as she tried to phrase her question.

"Sh-h-h. Don't try to talk. You'll tire yourself." The nurse laid a reassuring hand on Joni's shoulder. "You're in ICU—the Intensive Care Unit. You've had surgery, and we're taking good care of you. So don't worry. Try to go back to sleep if you can."

Over the next few days Joni gradually became more aware of her surroundings. She learned that the canvas sandwich she was strapped into wasn't really a bed; it was called a Stryker Frame. And every couple of hours two nurses or orderlies would flip her 180 degrees to keep her from getting bedsores.

But the frame and the tongs that clamped and held her head still gave her only two views: the floor or the ceiling.

She did learn she was in an eight-bed ICU unit. And as the hours blurred into days, by watching and listening, she got to know a little about her roommates.

The man handcuffed in the bed next to hers had shot his wife and then tried to kill himself. A woman in one of the beds moaned all night and begged the nurses for ice cream and cigarettes. A young girl named Judy was in a coma as a result of a car accident.

A young man named Tom was there because of a diving accident much like Joni's. With the help of nurses and family visitors, who served as note takers and couriers, they began to send messages back and forth.

Joni felt a kinship with Tom. She knew he had broken his neck and was in worse shape than she was. He couldn't even breathe on his own. He had a respirator that breathed for him by pumping air in and out of his lungs. At night, when the activity slowed down on the ward and there was nothing to keep her attention but the moaning and groaning of the others in the ward, Joni found the rhythm of

Tom's respirator a reassuring sound. As long as she heard it, she knew he was okay.

Then one night, that whoosh sound stopped. The sudden silence seemed as loud as an explosion. Joni's voice cracked as she called for help. She could hear nurses running to Tom's bedside.

"His respirator is down! We need a new one. Stat!"

Joni heard footsteps running out of the room and down the hall. There was a scraping metallic sound as the oxygen unit was moved. Somebody in the nurse's station phoned for emergency help. Within moments the ward was crowded with people.

"Tom! Can you hear me, Tom?" a doctor called. "Where's that other resuscitator?" he snapped.

"The orderly had to go downstairs for another unit," a nurse explained. "He's on his way."

"Keep up the mouth-to-mouth then."

The doors of the elevator down the hall opened. Joni heard running footsteps and the rattle of equipment approaching the ward. "I've got a unit," someone said. "You want to make room."

"Never mind," came the reply. "We've lost him."

Joni felt the flesh on the back of her neck crawl. Tom was dead. She wanted to scream, but she didn't. That night she did not fall asleep easily. She was afraid that she too might never wake up.

When another man in a Stryker Frame died a few days later, Joni decided the ICU ward was a room for the dying. She felt her own life was now a fragile thing—not something she could take for granted ever again.

One time not long after that, when the nurses flipped her over on her stomach, Joni fainted and stopped breathing. But within minutes, the hospital staff revived her. "We're going to take good care of you, Joni," one doctor reassured her. And after that, while every turn was still a frightening experience for her, she realized the nurses and the orderlies did seem to be more careful than before.

However, fears about dying continued to plague her for some time. Yet sometimes they were pushed to the back of her mind during visits from family and friends who came as often as they could. But Joni felt bad whenever visitors came while she was facedown in her Stryker Frame because that meant they had to get down on the floor for her to see them. She felt especially terrible having her mom and dad crawl under her in order to carry on a face-to-face conversation.

One day in August Joni's boyfriend, Dick, came to visit while she was lying facedown. When he slid underneath her, she noticed he was wearing a jacket. Since the day was sunny and warm, she wondered what was up.

"I've just run up all nine floors," he gasped.

Joni laughed. "Why didn't you use the elevator?"

"This is why!" He opened his jacket and pulled out a squirming little puppy. It crawled all over Dick, licking his face and barking in an excited and surprisingly loud "yip, yip, yip" that threatened to alert the entire hospital.

"Quiet, pooch!" Dick begged. "You want to get us kicked out?"

He lifted the puppy up to Joni's face where she could feel his fuzzy warmth and laugh as he licked her cheek.

"He's beautiful, Dickie," Joni exclaimed. "I'm so glad you brought him."

A nurse surprised them by walking into the room. "I thought I heard something," she exclaimed in mock seriousness. "How'd you get him past the Gestapo in the lobby?"

"I came up the back stairs," Dick confessed. "You aren't going to turn us in, are you?"

She grinned. "Who? Me?" The nurse picked up and cuddled the puppy, then put him back down on Dick's chest. "I never saw a thing," she declared as she headed out the door for other duties.

Joni and her boyfriend played with that puppy for nearly an hour before Dick had to leave. "I'll take the stairs again," he told her. "Otherwise they may search me every time I come for a visit."

They laughed. And Dick snuck out with the puppy back under his jacket.

The next day Joni had a bone scan and myelo-gram done. The bone scan was nothing more than taking a picture of her spine. But the myelogram wasn't nearly so simple. First, a sample of her spinal fluid was tapped and replaced with dye using a couple of giant, six-inch needles. Then she was turned upside down and put in several other posi-tions under a fluoroscope while the medics ran their tests. When they finished, as much of the dye as possible was drawn out with another long needle.

This painful procedure often results in such horrible headaches that Joni was sedated for several days simply as a precaution.

When her physician came by later to see how she was doing, Joni demanded to know, "What's wrong with me, Dr. Sherrill?"

His calm reply gave no hint as to the seriousness of her condition. "Don't you remember, Joni? You have a lesion of the spinal cord at the fourth and fifth cervical levels caused by a fracture-dislocation."

Joni thought she knew what that meant. "You mean I broke my neck?"

"Yes."

When she was younger, Joni had read the book *Black Beauty*. A man in that story fell off a horse and broke his neck. He died. Tom had broken his neck. He died too.

"That means I'll die," she said to Dr. Sherrill.

"Not necessarily," he replied. "It's true many people don't survive accidents of this nature. But the fact you have survived four weeks now means you've more than likely passed the crisis."

Joni thought about Tom and the other ICU patient who had died. "I guess I'm lucky," she said. But she didn't feel so lucky strapped tight in her Stryker Frame, hurting and homesick.

"You were lucky indeed," Dr. Sherrill agreed. "And strong. When you get a little stronger, I want to perform fusion surgery."

"What's that?" Joni wanted to know. "In plain English."

"Your spinal cord is severed," the doctor explained. "We have to fuse the bones back together."

Back together! Joni thought. *That means he's gonna fix my broken neck! Before long I'll be back on my feet. That's the first good news I've heard since my accident.*

"When do you want to do the surgery?" she asked.

"As soon as possible," he told her.

"Great! Let's do it!" Joni couldn't wait for the surgery.

Joni may have been too excited to hear much that was said about the proposed operation. So after the surgery, when she was wheeled into a regular hospital room instead of the ICU ward, she thought,

That's a good sign. I must be getting better or they'd keep me where I was in the ICU.

Her parents were waiting for Joni in her room. They were still there when Dr. Sherrill stopped by to check on his patient. "Everything went fine," he said, anticipating their first question. "The surgery was a complete success."

All the Earecksons gave a big sigh of relief as the doctor went on to tell Joni, "There will be many more difficult days ahead, Joni. And the toughest part may be in your mind—as your friends go off to college and the novelty of this wears off. Your friends will have other interests and will stop coming by so often. You need to prepare yourself for that."

Joni didn't know why he sounded so concerned. None of those things mattered now that the surgery had been successful. "I know it will take time," she assured the doctor, "but I'll get better."

"How much time are we talking about, Dr. Sherrill?" Mr. Eareckson asked.

Before he could respond, Joni's mother added, "You're talking about Joni's friends going off to college this fall. It sounds like you're saying Joni won't be able to go. Should we wait until next semester?"

"Mrs. Eareckson," he replied slowly, as if surprised by the question. "I'm afraid college will be out of the question for Joni."

"Y-you mean you don't know how soon Joni will walk again?"

"Walk? I'm afraid you don't understand," the doctor said. "Joni's injury is permanent. The fusion surgery didn't change that."

The word *permanent* slammed into Joni's mind like a bullet in the heart.

Seeing Joni's and her parents' shock, the doctor tried to encourage them by saying, "While she may not be able to walk, we're hopeful that in time Joni will be able to get the use of her hands back."

But Joni couldn't get past that horrible word *permanent*. Could it be true? Would she never be able to walk again?

FAITH, HOPE, AND FEAR

Joni had heard what her doctor said. But she didn't want to believe it. She insisted Dr. Sherrill was wrong. She told her family, her friends, her nurses, and anyone else who would listen that she would get better and stronger ... that with God's help, she would walk again.

She set out to prove it by being positive and optimistic about everything with everyone. Instead of focusing on her own problems, she thought about others in the hospital who were worse off than she was. She worked hard to cheer up her family and friends when they came to visit her. And she made an effort to be more pleasant with the hospital staff.

She hoped to kindle their hope and faith. But she was also afraid people would quit coming to see her if she seemed bitter and complaining. So she worked at cheerfulness.

"My, you're in a good mood today," one of her day-shift nurses observed.

"Why not?" Joni responded. "It's a gorgeous day!"

"It's raining, Joni!"

"Not on me." She grinned. "I'm snug as a bug."

Many of Joni's visitors remarked on her inspiring courage and faith. But it proved difficult to continue acting upbeat and positive when the days and weeks dragged by and she didn't get better or stronger. In fact, she grew weaker because she wasn't eating; just the thought of food turned her stomach.

Visitors were the one thing she looked forward to. But one day two of her girlfriends from high school came to visit. They hadn't seen her since the accident. So when they walked into Joni's room, they seemed surprised by the Stryker Frame and all the other equipment. When they walked up beside the bed, they didn't say anything at first. They acted awkward and seemed to avoid looking at the tongs pressing into the sides of Joni's skull.

"Hi." Joni greeted them with a smile. "I'm sorry I can't turn my head to see you, but if you'll . . ."

"Oh, Joni!" choked one of the girls.

"Oh, my God . . ." whispered the other.

There was a long, awkward moment of silence before one, then the other, ran for the door. Joni heard one of them retch and vomit in the hall as the second girl began to sob.

No one else had reacted like that. Joni wondered what was going on. *Maybe they just don't like hospitals. Or is it something else?*

Joni was afraid to find out. But a few days later, when her good friend Jackie was reading aloud some of her cards and mail, Joni looked at her and said, "Jackie, bring me a mirror."

"Why?" she asked.

"I just want you to get me a mirror! Please."

"Okay," Jackie agreed. "I'll bring one next time I come."

"I mean now! Get one from the nurse."

"Why don't we wait, Joni? I'll bring you your pretty dresser set from home."

"Jackie!" Joni was getting angry. "Bring me a mirror! Now!"

Jackie slowly edged to the door and came back a couple minutes later with a mirror. But her hands shook, and she blinked nervously as she held it in front of her friend.

Joni screamed. Jackie jumped and nearly dropped the mirror.

"It's ghastly!" Joni exclaimed as she began to cry. "Oh, God, how can you do this to me?" she prayed aloud, tears streaming down her face.

The face Joni saw in the mirror seemed scarcely human. Her eyes were dark, sunk in their sockets, bloodshot and glassy. Medication had blackened her teeth. Her weight had dropped from 125 to 80. She looked like a skeleton covered with sickly yellow skin. Her shaved head somehow made it all worse.

Joni felt like vomiting herself. "Take it away! I never want to look in a mirror again."

Jackie began to cry with her. "I'm sorry, Joni, I didn't want you to see."

"I can't take it anymore," Joni told her friend. "I'm dying, Jackie. Look at me. Why do they let me suffer like this?"

"I . . . I don't know, Joni."

"Jackie, you've got to help me. They're keeping me alive and it's not right. I'm dying anyway. Why can't they just let me die? Jackie, please, help me!"

"But how?"

"I don't know," Joni answered. "Give me something. An overdose of pills. Or you could slit my wrist. I wouldn't even feel it."

Jackie's eye widened. "You mean you want me to kill you?"

"Yes . . . I mean, no!" how could Joni explain. "You wouldn't be killing me. You'd just be helping me die sooner and end the suffering. If I could move, I'd do it myself."

Jackie began to sob. "I can't, Joni. I just can't!"

Joni didn't say anymore then. But several times when she felt especially frustrated and depressed, she would beg Jackie to help her commit suicide. It made her angry that she couldn't do it herself.

From that time on, Jackie tried to help Joni look better when guests came. And Jackie tried everything she could think of to take her friend's mind off her discouraging situation. "You'll be better soon, Joni," she promised. "Remember, the Lord says he will never allow us to suffer more than we can humanly bear."

"Oh, yeah?" Joni grunted. She didn't want to hear that. She wasn't even sure she believed it, especially when her suffering seemed to only get worse.

The medication and her paralysis made Joni much more sensitive to light and sound than most people. So she made Jackie and the nurses keep the shades drawn and the door to her room closed to keep out light and noise. Still, she could hear conversations going on out in the hall and in other rooms. It grated on her nerves.

One day as Jackie was moving a fan, she dropped it. The sound, as it clattered on the tile floor, felt like an explosion going off inside Joni's head.

Joni screamed and cursed at her friend and called her names. Immediately, she felt terrible and tried to apologize. "Jackie, you're such a close friend. I take you for granted. I yell at you all the time when I really feel mad at God. I can't yell at Mom and Dad because they're already suffering so much. And I'm afraid to take the chance of losing Dick by yelling at him. But that means I'm always taking it out on you. And I'm really sorry."

"That's okay," Jackie said, smiling. "I know you don't mean it. Besides, what are friends for?"

Every time Dick came to the hospital, he tried to cheer Joni up. But when he reminded her how the Bible said, "All things work together for good . . . even your accident, Joni," she didn't want to hear it.

"I've already been in this stupid hospital for more than a month," she complained, "and I haven't seen very much good! I can't sleep at night because of the noise and the nightmares and hallucinations caused by the drugs they give me. I can't move! I'm stuck in this dumb Stryker Frame. Tell me, Dickie, what's good about any of this?"

"I . . . I don't know, Joni." He paused for a moment before he went on. "But I just think we should claim God's promise. Let's trust him that it will all work out for good," he said quietly and patiently. "Want me to read you something else?"

"No. . . . I'm sorry. I didn't mean to jump on you like that. I guess I'm not really trusting the Lord, am I?"

"It's all right." Dick was lying beneath her Stryker Frame so Joni saw the tears well up in his eyes. After he left that evening, she determined again to be more positive. She told herself, *If I can show God that I have more faith, maybe then he will help me get better.*

So when the doctor told Mr. Eareckson the family's insurance wouldn't cover all the medical bills, Joni said, "Don't worry, Dad. God will provide what we need."

When Dr. Sherrill warned her that paralysis is psychologically harder on an active, athletic person, she told him, "God will help me."

When her physical therapist told her she needed to get stronger before she could be transferred to Greenoaks Rehabilitation Hospital, Joni took that as another chance to show her faith and confidence. "That's where I'll learn to walk again." The therapist just smiled.

For almost a month, Joni and her nurses and doctors worked to get her ready for the transfer. When the day finally came and she'd said her goodbyes to the hospital staff, two orderlies wheeled her outside to the ambulance that would take her to Greenoaks.

The moment a rush of sweet-smelling outside air tickled her nose, Joni exclaimed, "Oh, wow! Wait a minute, please. Stop right here!" She breathed deeply and asked the orderlies, "Do you smell that air?"

One of them laughed. "Yeah. It sure is polluted."

Joni breathed deeply. She thought it was wonderful.

She asked the driver to keep the windows open so she could enjoy the autumn air. Summer was gone. The stores they passed were decorated for Halloween. The trees were red and gold and orange.

Trying not to think about the whole season she'd lost since the accident, Joni tried to picture Greenoaks in her mind. She imagined a beautiful colonial building with tall, white columns and sweeping green lawns with towering oak trees.

But when they pulled into the driveway, Greenoaks Rehabilitation Hospital looked more like a factory.

"Here we are," announced the driver.

"Yeah." Joni couldn't hide her disappointment.

"Anything wrong?"

"No . . . I guess not," she said. "I guess when you build some place up in your mind, it can never really live up to your expectations. Y' know?"

The attendant nodded. "Don't worry. They do good work here. They have several girls your age. I think you'll like it."

"I hope so," she told him. But Joni suddenly wasn't so sure about Greenoaks. She wasn't so sure about anything anymore.

AT GREENOAKS REHAB CENTER

Joni's parents were waiting for her when she got to Greenoaks. When they didn't stay long, Joni knew they were as disappointed as she was. She suspected they left in a hurry because they didn't want her to see them cry.

The inside of Greenoaks wasn't what Joni had imagined either. The old building's halls seemed dark and depressing. Everywhere she looked, Joni saw people slouched in wheelchairs or strapped into Stryker Frames. She didn't see any patients walking—no one who looked *healed*.

Four other girls shared a small ward with her. So as soon as she arrived, she introduced herself. "Hi! I'm Joni Eareckson."

"Joni Eareckson!" One of the girls repeated the name with contempt and then swore. "Joni

Eareckson. Joni Eareckson. That name is all I heard at City Hospital. Joni this, Joni that. I could puke!"

Stunned by the bitterness in her roommate's voice, Joni recovered enough to smile and say, "Oh, I didn't know I had a fan club here."

That broke the ice. The other girls laughed. "You'll have to excuse Ann," one of them said. "She's new here too. She was in City Hospital while you were there. But I guess she wasn't the model patient you were. I'm B. J. The girl in the bed over there is Denise.

"Hi. Pardon me if I don't get up," Denise said.

"Yeah," Joni joked back. "I know the un-feel-ing."

"And this is Betty." B. J. motioned with the flop of a useless arm toward a petite and pretty African-American girl who seemed younger than everyone else.

"Hi, Betty." Joni smiled.

Betty looked up and nodded slightly.

Ann evidently needed no further introduction.

B. J. filled Joni in on everyone. She had a broken neck like Joni. Betty had a blood clot on her spine. Denise had MS, or multiple sclerosis.

"How long have you been here?" Joni asked B. J.

"Two years."

Two years! B. J. was still paralyzed and in bed. Joni didn't even want to think about being at Greenoaks that long.

Later that night Joni lay in her Stryker Frame trying to get to sleep. But she felt too depressed and bitter. She tried to pray—but she couldn't. She tried to think of some encouraging Bible promises—but nothing seemed reassuring.

She decided no matter how frustrated and bitter she felt, she would be pleasant. At least on the surface. She wasn't going to be like Ann and drive everyone away. *I need my friends. Without them, I'll lose my mind,* Joni thought. No matter how bitter she was, she determined never to let it show.

"That's a good idea," B. J. said the next day when Joni told her what she'd been thinking. "You won't get much sympathy in here because everyone is pretty much the same. In fact, you'd be smart not to make many friends here."

"Why?" Joni wanted to know.

B. J. explained that the hospital wasn't at all like real life. "Since everyone is the same here, give or take an arm or a leg, it's comfortable. Once you get enough sitting-up time to get out, you can't wait to get back here—because it's easier here. No hassling about braces, wheelchairs, and stuff. That makes it hard to want to leave.

"The people on the street seem to think that since your legs are paralyzed, your brain must be too. So they treat ya like a dummy. Which is why everyone comes back here complaining and comparing injuries, but content because they fit in here. They feel at home. You'll be the same way if you make all your friends here.

"And just because it's easier here doesn't mean it's better. It isn't. I know. I've been here two years! Whatever you do, keep your friends on the outside."

Every new day at Greenoaks brought the same old routine. Joni remained confined to bed because of bedsores. She had lost so much weight that her bones had rubbed through her skin and made ugly, raw, oozing sores. A nurse would feed her every morning and then empty the urine from her catheter bag. Then the nurse would adjust the round mirror over Joni's bed so she could watch TV.

About noon she'd be fed and "emptied" again. Then more TV in the afternoon. Mornings were game shows. Afternoons were soap operas. Then in the evenings there'd be another meal and emptying of her urine bag followed by more TV watching until lights out. Every day seemed like a boring photocopy of the one before.

Eat, sleep, watch TV. That was pretty much it—one continuous cycle. And Joni had to learn to eat and drink as quickly as possible. Because the staff always acted busy. They had other people to feed and other things to do.

One day Joni's sister Jay came for a visit. "What's that horrible smell?" she wanted to know.

"What smell?" Joni had been in the hospital so long she'd gotten used to all sorts of smells.

"Ugh! It's your hair, Joni. When was the last time they washed it?"

"Over a month ago, back when I was at City Hospital," Joni admitted.

"That's awful!" Jay announced. "It stinks so bad we've got to do something about it."

She quickly collected a basin and soap and figured out how to manage to shampoo the hair of someone strapped in a Stryker Frame.

"Oh, it feels so good," Joni exclaimed.

"Me next!" called out Denise. "Wash my hair, Jay. Please!"

"Me too!" B. J. and Betty said at the same time.

So Jay washed, set, and brushed all their hair, every week. Until hospital regulations put an end to it.

Joni was grateful when PT—physical therapy—became part of her daily routine. At least it made for more variety in her life.

To begin with, the physical therapist came to her room every day to exercise her arms and legs to keep the muscles from withering up and causing all kinds of complications. "It keeps the muscles elastic," the therapist explained. "And that's good."

After a few weeks, Joni went to the PT center for two hours of work a day. The room reminded her of a torture chamber in an old horror movie. There were many bizarre-looking machines for stretching, pulling, and bending useless arms, legs, and bodies. But Joni welcomed the work. As she watched other patients struggling to master crutches and walkers, she told herself, *This is where I'm going to learn how to walk again.*

But first she had to learn to sit up. And that proved to be more difficult than she could ever have imagined.

First they fastened her to a tiltboard and gradually lifted her head while lowering her feet. She was hardly above horizontal when she felt blood rushing out of her head and waves of nausea sweeping over her.

"Stop! Don't go any higher! I can't take it," Joni sobbed. After six months of lying in a horizontal position, just a few seconds with her head raised was more than she could stand.

"Oh, Joe. I thought I was going to faint," she told her therapist. "Won't I ever be able to sit up?"

"Sure, Joni," he assured her. "It just takes time. By Thanksgiving, we'll have you sitting in a chair." And sure enough, they worked longer and longer each day until Joni could sit up without blacking out or feeling sick to her stomach.

★

Another one of Joni's regular visitors during this time was a friend named Diana. They knew each other from high school and a Christian youth group called Young Life. Diana was always so positive. And each time she came, she'd have some new encouragement from the Bible.

One day she told Joni, "Listen to this! It's from John 16:23–24: 'I assure you that whatever you ask the Father in my name, he will give you. Up to now you have asked nothing in my name; ask now, and you will receive, that your joy may be overflowing.' Isn't that great?"

"Yeah, it really is," Joni replied. "Hey, maybe God is doing something special. Did you hear about our church?"

"Church?" Diana asked. "No, what's happening?"

Joni told her about an all-night prayer service the Eareksons' church was planning just for her and about the tingling sensation she had in her fingers during PT. She told her friend she just knew God was beginning to heal her.

But the morning after the healing service, Joni didn't wake up healed. So she told herself God was going to work slowly and naturally and not in some big, miraculous way. And when her parents and friends came to visit her, she hid her disappointment and impatience.

"The Lord is going to heal me," she promised everyone. "Let's just keep praying and trusting."

"Oh, Joni," someone would gush. "You're so brave. I wish I had your faith!"

Joni always smiled sweetly. But under her breath, she prayed that God would hurry up and heal her.

★

By December, Joni was still weak, thin, and covered with bedsores. But her hard work in physical therapy had paid off with enough sitting-up time that the doctors said she could go home for one day. So, wearing the new blonde wig Jay had given her, Joni went home to be with her family on Christmas Day.

Her mom had decorated the house for the holidays. A big pine tree and a hospital bed were set up in the dining room so she wouldn't miss a thing. But the sights, sounds, and smells of celebration seemed almost too much for her. She had to half sit, half lie on the bed.

"Please, Mom," Joni asked. "Will you cover me?"

While she'd felt almost human again wearing a new suit and wig, she didn't want other people to look at her thin, useless legs. And she didn't want to look at them either. They reminded her that everything was so different this Christmas. No shopping for presents. No sledding. No caroling for the neighbors. No going to church with the family. She enjoyed the day with her family and Dick. But thinking back to other Christmases, she couldn't help feeling sad at how much had changed.

To make matters worse, after she returned to the hospital, they told her she wouldn't be going home again anytime soon. Sitting up so long had opened the sores on her back and hips where her bones protruded through her skin. She would have to go back in her Stryker Frame until they healed over again.

During that winter, Dick hitchhiked the sixty miles from the University of Maryland as often as he could. But Joni could tell the strain was getting to him. Coming to see her so often meant less time to study. His grades had suffered. He'd even lost his football scholarship.

Joni loved having him come to visit, but she knew she wasn't being fair to him. "We're holding on to the past, Dickie," she told him one day. "We can't go back to our high school days."

As usual, Dickie tried to cheer her up. "Things will get better."

"No," she cried. "I'll never get better. Can't you see that?"

In fact, things seemed to get worse. Joni's sores didn't heal. And doctors insisted surgery would be the only way to correct the problem. So in June she went back to City Hospital for the operations. The doctors chiseled off and smoothed down the sharp edges of the bones that caused the problems. After she was stitched up and bandaged, Joni was taken back to Greenoaks.

When the old bedsores and the new sutures finally healed, the day came when one of Joni's favorite orderlies lifted her out of the Stryker Frame, gently placed her on a bed, and helped her to slowly sit up.

"Take it nice and slow, Joni. Don't want ya to get dizzy and pass out. Right?"

"Right," Joni echoed.

"Easy now."

"How about that, Earl," Joni said with a grin. "I'm sitting up again." It felt so good.

Earl didn't say anything. Instead he picked her up and carried her back to the Stryker Frame.

"Hey, leave me in bed, Earl," she demanded. "I've waited too long to sit up again. If you're worried about me passing out . . . "

"Sorry, Joni," Earl said. "I gotta put you back. Your backbone just busted the incision open. You're bleeding again. The operation didn't take."

A CREATIVE
TURNING POINT

Lying in the Stryker those next few weeks, Joni finally gave up all hope of ever walking again. Instead she began concentrating all her willpower on being able to use her hands again.

She figured if she just had use of her hands, she could care for herself. She could wash. Eat. Put on makeup. She wouldn't have to feel so helpless.

"You can use your mouth to do some of the things you'd normally do with your hands," her occupational therapist Chris Brown told her after Joni shared her plan. "You've seen other people in OT [occupational therapy] learn to write or type by holding a pencil or a stick in their mouths. You can learn too."

"No," Joni told her. "It's disgusting and degrading. I won't do it." If she did that it would be like giving up hope that she could ever use her hands again.

Dick and Diana still came to see her regularly. But when they wanted to share encouraging Scriptures with her, Joni quit listening. Her growing doubts about God were as deep as the resentment she felt about what had happened. She wondered who or what was God. *Certainly not a personal Being who cares for us,* she reasoned. *What's the use of believing when your prayers fall on deaf ears?*

So Joni began to read books about other philosophies and religions, trying to find something that helped. But when none of those things seemed to make sense, she began reading the Bible again. At night, when the lights were turned off and all the visitors had gone home, she would pray, "God, if I can't die, show me how to live, please!"

It may have been the most heartfelt prayer she'd ever prayed. For a while she wondered if he even heard it. Things only seemed to get worse.

One of the night-shift attendants, Mrs. Barber, acted like patients were a bother. Joni was scared of her and with good reason. She could be mean and insulting when no one else was around.

One night she came into the ward and angrily swept all of Joni's photographs off the top of the air conditioner. She swore and complained about not being able to work the air conditioner with all the stuff on it. Then she picked up a picture of Dick and said some truly insulting things about him.

When Joni protested, the woman walked over to the Stryker and hissed, "I ought to leave you like this until morning and not flip you at all." She gave a cruel smile. "But to show you what a nice person I am, I'll turn you right now."

Turning patients was supposed to be a two-person job. But Mrs. Barber didn't care. Without even checking to make sure Joni's arms were tucked in, she gave such a violent flip that one of Joni's arms swung out, banging her hand on the metal frame.

Joni never felt any pain, but her hand swelled up and eventually turned black and blue. And when the angry woman left the room, Joni began to cry.

"I saw what she did, Joni," B. J. said. "You oughtta turn her in."

But Joni was afraid if she reported her, the woman would do something else—worse. The next day when Mrs. Eareckson came to visit, she asked about the bruised hand. Joni dismissed it as the result of an accident, but when the other girls told her what really happened, she stormed off and complained loudly to the supervisor.

Sure enough, late that night Mrs. Barber slipped into the darkened ward and leaned down with her face right next to Joni's. "If you ever say anything against me again ... you'll pay. Do you understand?"

Joni knew it wasn't an idle threat. She was terrified.

There were a lot of nice people who worked at Greenoaks. But everyone on staff seemed overworked.

One day her friend Diana stopped by to say she'd decided to drop out of college for a while. She wanted to volunteer her time at the hospital to help take better care of Joni. There was no talking her out of it. "I've prayed about it," she said, "and I believe it's what God wants me to do."

Diana told Joni she thought it sounded like a good idea to learn to write with her mouth. "But I'm making good progress in PT," Joni told her. "I'm gonna get back the use of my hands."

"But what if you don't?" Diana asked.

Joni didn't want to think about that. Besides, Diana was the one always telling her she needed to trust God. Why would God keep her in a wheelchair and take away the use of her hands too? It didn't make sense.

"Maybe you shouldn't think about the future just yet. Why not take one step at a time?" Diana said.

Joni decided maybe her friend was right. As long as she was in a rehab hospital, maybe she ought to concentrate on being rehabilitated.

So the next day Joni told Chris Brown she wanted to start learning how to do things with her mouth. "How do I start?"

"Hold this pencil in your mouth," Chris told her. "Grip it with your teeth like this." She put a pencil in her own mouth and then stuck a second one in Joni's.

"Okay. Good. See how easy it is. Uh . . . not so tight. You'll get writer's cramp in your jaw. Hold it just firmly enough not to drop it, just tight enough to control it. Like this, see?"

"Mmmm."

Chris first taught her to make lines and circles and other shapes. They all looked pretty shaky at first. But after many hours of practice, Joni began to get more control. Finally, she began working on the letters of the alphabet. And with real effort and concentration, she actually wrote a letter to her parents. It was short. And the letters were big and looked like a kindergartner's scrawl—big, awkward squiggles. But it was writing, and it made her feel like she was making progress.

In September, more than a year after her accident, Joni went to Kernans Hospital for another operation to try to solve the bedsore problem. This time the surgery was a success. But she still had to spend the next fifteen days lying face down in a Stryker Frame while the incisions on her back and hips healed.

On October 15, Joni celebrated her seventeenth birthday. Her family and friends came to help celebrate. But the best present of all was being turned face up again—and knowing that because the operation was a success, she could begin looking forward to getting a wheelchair.

Many of her paralyzed friends at Greenoaks had gotten their own chairs and finally been able to go home. That encouraged Joni enough that she jumped back into her own therapy with new determination. She wanted to get out and go home too—the sooner, the better!

Since Joni seemed so willing to do new things, her occupational therapist, Chris Brown, suggested, "Now that you can write pretty well, why not do something artistic?"

"Artistic?" Joni wasn't sure what she meant.

"You've shown me drawings you used to do. You enjoy creative things. You could paint these ceramic disks. They make nice gifts."

"I don't know . . . " Joni hesitated. She watched another quadriplegic patient slopping paint on a piece of clay using a paintbrush. It seemed useless. It reminded her of kindergarten again.

"Oh, come on. Try it," Chris urged her.

So Joni did. She spilled globs of color in clumsy designs on the clay disks. It was discouraging at first, and she hated every minute of it. But when the disks came out of the kiln, they didn't look half bad. And with practice, like with writing, she got better.

Over the next few weeks, she created several Christmas gifts for her family and friends. Joni didn't know what they would think of the candy dishes. But at least she'd done them herself.

Then one day Chris brought her some moist clay. "I want you to draw a picture on it," she told Joni.

"How?"

The therapist gave her a stylus to hold in her mouth. "Try this."

Joni didn't know what to draw.

"Why not do something you like," Chris suggested.

Carefully, Joni gauged the distance from her mouth to the soft clay, poked at it with the pointed stick, then tried to etch a line. She told Chris, "The last time I drew anything was on our family trip out West just before the accident. All during my childhood, Daddy encouraged me to draw. He's a self-taught artist." Out West she had filled her sketchpad with drawings of mountains, people, horses, and other animals.

Remembering those drawings, Joni etched out a simple line drawing of a cowboy and his horse on the clay.

Chris was amazed at Joni's first attempt. "You've got real talent, Joni. We should have been doing this before. You need to get back to your art."

"But that was when I had hands," Joni protested.

The therapist shook her head. "Hands are just tools. That's all. The talent is in the brain. Once you've practiced, you can do as well with your mouth as you did with your hands."

"Wow! Really?" Joni asked.

"Yeah! Want to try?"

"Sure! Let's do it."

That day turned out to be a real turning point in Joni's life. Being able to express herself in a creative way again gave her reason to hope. It also gave her another reason to trust.

Once again she began to believe that God understood her. He had made her a creative person. He was providing a way to express that creativity.

She also began to realize that Jesus himself could certainly understand her situation. When his hands and feet were nailed to the cross and he suffered that horrible, painful death, he had been helpless. Paralyzed really. He understood!

So when Joni had a bad day—no one came to visit, therapy didn't go well—whenever she got discouraged and wanted to cry but couldn't because she wouldn't be able to wipe away the tears or blow her nose, she would picture Jesus standing right beside her in the room, speaking to her in a strong but tender voice, "Lo, I am with you always. And if I loved you enough to die for you, don't you think I ought to know best how to run your life now that you are paralyzed." Jesus' presence seemed so real to Joni that it gave her the comfort she needed to make it through the longest nights and the darkest days.

She believed God really did understand—that he still had a plan for her life. That's why she began to sign "PTL"—"Praise the Lord"—on all her drawings. She knew God cared for her. He was answering her prayers. He would help her learn how to live again.

7

RANCHOS LOS AMIGOS

Joni was encouraged to see that she was improving and growing stronger. She was looking forward to going home again for the Christmas holidays. This time she planned to stay several days.

In early December, her parents told Joni about a new hospital they had heard about in Los Angeles. "It's called Ranchos Los Amigos," her dad said.

"They've been able to teach people to regain the use of their arms and legs," her mother added. "Even so-called impossible cases."

That sounded great to Joni. "Can we go there?"

"Your mom and I couldn't be with you," her dad said. "But your sister Jay wants to go. She could get an apartment nearby. We're checking on all that now. We should hear soon."

"Wow! Wouldn't that be some Christmas present!" Joni exclaimed.

Christmas was great. Joni could hardly believe it had been a whole year since she'd been home. The familiar surroundings felt good to her. And when Dick asked her to go out to a movie with him, she was thrilled.

But as much as Joni wanted everything to be normal again, it was impossible. During the movie, when Dick put his arm around her and squeezed her affectionately, she didn't even notice. Finally he asked, "Don't you feel that?"

"What?"

He squeezed her again. "This."

"I'm sorry," Joni said, embarrassed. She wanted to feel his touch.

On their drive home later, Dick had to stop suddenly and Joni flew forward and hit her head on the dash. She couldn't catch herself or pick herself up. She wasn't hurt. But again she was embarrassed.

Dick felt terrible. "Why didn't I remember to hold you?" he scolded himself.

"I'm okay," Joni told him. "Please don't blame yourself. It just takes getting used to. Don't let it spoil our evening. Okay?"

When they got back to the Eareckson home and Dick wheeled her into the house, Joni thanked him. "I really had fun. This is the first time I've done anything this normal for a year and a half. Thank you."

"It was fun," Dick agreed as he leaned down and kissed the top of her forehead. "Glad you enjoyed yourself."

But Joni knew it wasn't really like "old times." They were both still awkward and uncomfortable dealing with her chair. She wondered, *Will things ever seem normal again?*

Joni dreaded going back to Greenoaks after Christmas. "You don't have to," her dad told her. "We just learned Rancho Los Amigos has room. You can leave right after New Year's." He grinned.

Joni began to cry. "Oh, Daddy. I'm so happy! The Lord does answer prayer." *Rancho Los Amigos*, she said to herself. *That's where I will get back my hands.*

Remembering how disappointed she was when she first saw Greenoaks, Joni didn't try to imagine what Rancho Los Amigos might look like. But to her surprise, it was beautiful. And many of the staff were college students, working their way through school. So she had people her own age to talk to.

Her therapy started right away. And it did focus on the use of her hands.

She was fitted with forearm braces and quickly learned to raise and lower her arms by "throwing" certain muscles in her shoulders and back. Joni couldn't move her fingers or bend her wrists, so she couldn't pick up anything. But she did begin learning to feed herself with a bent spoon attached to her arm brace.

By swinging her arm, Joni could maneuver the spoon over her plate. Then by raising and lowering the spoon into the food, she could actually feed herself. The movements reminded her of a steam shovel. It wasn't very precise. In fact, she often spilled as much as she got into her mouth. But after a year and a half of depending on other people to feed her, being able to lift a bit of mashed potatoes into her own mouth seemed like a wonderful accomplishment.

Joni's parents stayed in California until she got settled into the new routine, and her sister Jay found an apartment near Rancho Los Amigos. One night about a week after her folks had gone home, Joni heard a loud commotion in the hall. Then she heard the voices; there was no mistaking them. Seconds later, Dick, Diana, and Jackie exploded into her room.

"I can't believe it!" Joni shrieked at her friends.

"We got lonesome," Dick said with a grin.

"Glad to see us?" asked Jackie.

"Oh, you guys! How'd you get here?"

"Drove all the way," Diana told her.

"Nonstop," Dick added. "That's why we're so grubby."

Visiting hours got stretched that night as Joni's friends told her all about their sudden decision to surprise her and recounted the highlights of their cross-country trip. The next day Joni thanked her doctor for letting her friends stay.

"I don't want anyone chasing your friends away," he told her. "In fact, I want them to come as often as they can."

"Really?"

"Sure," he said. "I hope they can observe you in all your therapy to learn as much as possible about you and your disability. Then they'll be better able to help take care of you when you go home."

"H-home?" Joni stammered. The word seemed a little too good to be true.

"I think you should set a realistic goal and plan on finishing here by April 15," the doctor told her.

"That's only three months," Joni replied. "Will I be ready?"

The doctor looked at her thoughtfully. "That will be up to you. Are you willing to work at it?"

Joni grinned. "Oh, wow! Am I!"

Now that she'd begun to feed herself, Joni's next big goal to work on was using a wheelchair by herself. Judy, one of the attendants, showed her how to make her chair move by throwing her arms against one of the eight knobs on the outside of the wheels. "Now I want you to drive to PT," she said.

"But my PT isn't scheduled till nine," Joni told her.

Judy just grinned. "Right."

It took Joni all of those two hours to make it thirty feet down the hall to the PT room. She was absolutely exhausted.

But Judy was waiting. "You did great," she said.

"Does everyone take this long?" Joni asked.

Judy nodded. "Especially at first. A lot of people give up. Some fall out of their chairs."

Joni practiced "driving" every day after that. Sometimes she veered into a wall and was stuck for who knows how long until one of the staff walked by and rescued her. But she soon improved enough to be assigned an electric wheelchair to use.

After that, Joni practically lived in her chair, which was operated by a little black box on the armrest with a joystick she could move with her arm brace. After almost two years of being confined to bed, it seemed wonderful to be able to get around on her own. She even went outside to roam the neighborhood around the hospital.

Soon she was racing her chair against Rick, another patient. There was a whirring sound as they sent their chairs speeding down the corridor in a "fifty-yard dash." The first race was a tie.

"We can't get up any real speed in here," Rick complained. "We've got to go farther. Let's race from this end of the building to the end of the hall, around the corner, to the front door.

"You're on!" Joni told him.

Judy and another attendant pretended not to notice what was going on. They turned and walked the other way.

"On your mark!" Joni called to Rick. "Get set. Go!"

The two were off—building up speed as they rolled side by side down the hall. Other patients stared or smiled as they sped past. First Rick's chair inched ahead. Then Joni's. Neck and neck they went into the far turn at the end of the hall. Joni was so determined to win that she took the turn without even slowing down.

But as she wheeled around the corner, there, right in front of her, was a nurse carrying a tray full of bottles and medicine. The surprised nurse froze. Joni screamed, "Look out!"

Too late! The tray went flying. Bottles and medicine crashed to the floor. And Joni's chair pinned the screaming nurse against the wall while Joni tried in vain to stop the motor by striking at the jammed control box. The wheels kept spinning. The nurse kept shrieking. Joni kept pounding clumsily at the controls. And all the while Rick laughed hysterically.

Joni didn't laugh for some time. The incident caused her to lose her driving privileges for a while. And when she got her chair back, she had to promise to keep it in low gear.

8

A THANKFUL HEART

When April 15, 1969, came, Joni's doctor told her she was ready to leave Rancho Los Amigos and return home. She had worked hard and reached all her rehab goals.

But Joni still had one big question she needed answered. "I've been working hard to get my hands back," she said. "Now I'm beginning to wonder if I ever will."

The doctor was bluntly honest with her. "No, Joni. You will never get your hands back. You might as well get used to the idea."

That was not what she'd hoped and prayed to hear. And she didn't feel ready to accept the fact that she would be a quadriplegic forever. Always dependent. Always helpless.

Tearfully she wrote Dick a letter. Part of what she said was:

"I can never be your wife .... God must have something else in mind for us. ... I hope we can go on being friends, Dickie .... But I want you to be free to date other girls and look for God to lead you to the right one. I can never be that woman ...."

She didn't sign it "Your Joni" like she always had before. This time she signed it just "Joni."

She was happy to be home again—at least on the outside. But on the inside, Joni's disappointment and discouragement made her bitter and angry again—because God hadn't answered her prayers and given her back her hands.

She had accepted the idea that she would never walk again. But she'd gone to California dreaming and believing she could learn to use her hands—so she could eventually drive a car, make meals, and put her arms around someone she loved. That she'd be able to drink a glass of water, bathe herself, brush her own hair, and put on her own makeup.

Now the terrible, painful truth began to sink in. She was going to be a quadriplegic for as long as she lived. And that depressed her.

Diana spent a lot of time helping to take care of Joni and trying to encourage her. "You can't give up, Joni," she insisted. "You've got to work with what you have left."

"I have nothing left," Joni told her friend.

"Don't give me that," Diana scolded. "There were people in the hospital with you who were blind, mute, deaf. Some had lost their minds. *They* had nothing left, Joni. But you have your mind, your voice, your eyes, your ears. You have everything you need."

Joni wasn't convinced.

Dick came to visit. He tried to get Joni to change her mind about breaking off their relationship. "I don't care if you're ever healed or not," he told her. "I want to marry you anyway."

Joni told him, "It wouldn't work. Sometimes my paralysis is too much for me to handle, let alone you."

"Sharing the burden would make it lighter for both of us," he said.

"That's romantic," Joni replied, "but it's not realistic."

Dick finally agreed. "Maybe you're right." But his eyes filled with tears as he said it.

Joni felt even more discouraged after that. She began spending more and more time sleeping or just daydreaming—thinking all the time about the way things used to be. When friends came out to the family farm to go riding, she would remember how much she used to love riding her horse. When she sat by a friend's pool, she would daydream about times when she used to go swimming. She spent more time living in the past than she did enjoying the present.

Until the day Diana helped snap her out of her depression. She actually shook her by the shoulders and shouted, "Joni, stop it! What's wrong? Are you sick? I was talking to you and you were just staring into space."

"Just leave me alone," Joni told her friend.

"You're trying to avoid reality, Joni," Diana told her. "It's time to face the truth. The past is dead. But you're alive."

"Am I?" Joni challenged her. "This isn't living."

But Diana refused to let Joni give up or feel sorry for herself. She'd scold her out of her fantasies whenever she caught Joni daydreaming. Still, Joni often tried to withdraw into herself.

One day her father asked, "What's the matter, honey?"

She told him she didn't know. "I feel discouraged and depressed. Just when I think I've got things under control, I go into another tailspin."

Her father assured her that he and her mother would do anything they could to help, no matter how long the adjustment took.

Joni sighed and admitted, "I guess what affects me most is being so helpless. Everywhere I look around the house, I see things you've built and created. When you're gone, we will have the beautiful buildings, paintings, sculpture, and art you left us—even the furniture you've made. It's really sad to think I won't be able to leave a legacy like yours."

Mr. Eareckson smiled lovingly at his daughter. "You've got it all wrong, honey. The things I've done with my hands don't mean anything. It's much more important to build character—to leave something of yourself behind. And you don't need hands to build character."

Joni thought a lot about what her father had said. While she still felt angry at God, part of her now believed there had to be some purpose, something he could make out of all that had happened to her. Maybe like her dad said, character was what really mattered.

But no matter how hard she tried, Joni couldn't imagine what God might be trying to show her. So she prayed: "Lord, I believe you have something planned for my life. But I need help understanding your will. So please, God, do something in my life to help me serve you and know what you want me to do."

The answer to that prayer didn't come in a way Joni would have ever expected. But not long afterward, Diana told her, "I want to bring a friend over to meet you."

"Who? Why?"

"His name is Steve Estes. He has a real love for God and a great knowledge of the Bible. He's a young guy. In fact, he's still in high school."

"High school?" Joni reacted. "Diana! He's a kid?"

She smiled. "Wait till you meet him."

Joni didn't have long to wait. Steve came over that evening. And the moment he walked in the door, she was impressed. Not just by his tall, dark-haired, green-eyed appearance, but by his open and confident manner. Her wheelchair often seemed to make first-time visitors feel awkward, leaving Joni feeling self-conscious. But Steve seemed so comfortable that she relaxed and enjoyed his company.

They started regularly studying the Bible together, and Steve helped her understand that she really needed to quit looking back at the past and concentrate on living for God in the present. It wasn't easy, but Joni got rid of as many reminders of the past as she could. She gave away her hockey and lacrosse sticks. She even sold her horse, Tumbleweed.

One day after they read 1 Thessalonians 5:18, "Give thanks in all circumstances, for this is God's will for you in Christ Jesus," Steve closed his Bible and said, "Joni, it's about time you got around to giving thanks for that wheelchair of yours."

"I can't do that," Joni told him. "I don't want to be a hypocrite. I'm not going to give thanks when I don't feel thankful."

Steve said, "Wait a minute, Joni. Read the verse again. It doesn't say you have to feel like a million bucks about everything. It says, 'Give thanks in all circumstances . . . .'"

So Joni gritted her teeth and, through her tears, she gave thanks. "Thank you, Lord, for my hospital bed, and for my wheelchair—even though I'd rather be able to get up and walk. Thank you that all my physical therapy is helping me. Lord, I'm grateful that when I write by holding a pencil between my teeth it no longer looks like chicken scratches . . . ."

As Joni began to pray that way every day, to give thanks in all her circumstances, she found that her attitude began to change. Her bitterness and anger began to dissolve away. As she thanked God, she actually began to *feel* thankful.

9

SMALL BEGINNINGS

Steve Estes asked Joni to speak to the youth group at his church. She told him she wouldn't know what to say. He encouraged her to talk about her experience and the spiritual lessons she had learned.

But the thought of speaking to fifteen teenagers terrified her. And when the time came, she was even more nervous than she'd imagined possible.

"I ... uh ... I'm Joni Eareckson ... and ... uh ..." her mind went blank. She tried again. "I ... uh ... I want to tell you ... uh ... what Jesus means to me. Uh ... you know ... I've had lots of ... uh ... problems. But ... uh ... I ... I mean he ... he's been faithful. And uh ... I hope you know him as I do."

Her throat felt dry. Her face turned red with embarrassment because she couldn't think of anything more to add. So she just looked down and said nothing. After a long, awkward silence, Steve picked up on what Joni had said, made some comments of his own, and did a great job of tying it all together.

Afterward, Joni told him, "I don't ever want to do anything like that again as long as I live."

Steve tried to assure her he'd stammered and not known what to say the first time he spoke to a group. "You just need a little experience," he told Joni. "And maybe you could go to college and get some training. You could enroll at the University of Maryland. They have quite a few students in wheelchairs."

Joni had pretty much given up the idea of college. But she told Steve, "Maybe you're right."

He grinned and nodded.

"All right," Joni told him. "If Jay and Diana can help, I'll go to college this fall."

In September, Joni began some public-speaking classes at the university. Jay or Diana would go with her and take notes. Her speeches were about things she knew—how to relate to people with disabilities, accepting her wheelchair, and her Christian experience.

People seemed interested in what she had to say, and that gave her confidence. Deep inside, it also gave her a sense that God was preparing her for something yet to come.

Steve and Joni continued to have regular Bible studies in her home. She and Diana and three guys who came to those meetings formed a singing group that eventually got to be good enough to be asked to perform for youth groups and church services. About this same time, Joni was asked to serve as a volunteer counselor for a nearby Young Life club, where she began to see that her own experience and the spiritual lessons she was learning in her life could apply to other people. She quickly realized that many of the teenagers she worked with were restless, uncertain, and searching—just like she'd been. She quickly concluded that everyone has limitations and handicaps. And many of the lessons she'd learned about accepting herself and living in a wheelchair could help people with more common handicaps such as shyness, being overweight, feeling different or lonely, or coming from a troubled family.

Joni helped a lot of young people see that if God could help her accept and deal with her challenges, he could certainly help them. And that next summer, she and Jay served as counselors for a Young Life camp at a place called Frontier Ranch, located in the central Colorado Rockies.

As Steve Estes and other friends went away to college, and especially as several friends, including Diana, fell in love and got married, Joni began to think back on her relationship with Dick. She asked herself, *What if . . . ?* She wondered if she would ever find a man who could love her and deal with her circumstances. She began to pray, "Lord, please bring someone into my life to fill this emptiness."

Soon after that, she met Donald Bertolli at a Young Life leadership conference. They hit it off so well that she soon believed Donald was God's answer to her prayers. He took her out to eat. They talked for hours. They went on trail hikes, where he'd push her wheelchair as far as it could go and then carry her the rest of the way to the top of the hill. They'd have a picnic on a blanket and enjoy the view. One time at the beach, he pushed her wheelchair right out into the surf. When she screamed, "What are you doing?" he picked her up and carried her out into the breakers until they were both laughing and sopping wet.

What she loved best about Donald was the way he made her feel "normal" again—for the first time since her accident. He never let the wheelchair get in the way of treating her like he would any woman he liked.

Joni enjoyed the attention. But she worried about the growing affection she felt for Donald. He told her that he loved her, and they talked about the possibility of marriage. They also began to pray that Joni would be healed. Eventually Joni came to the conclusion that a healing wasn't going to happen, and they stopped talking about a future together.

When they finally broke up, Joni's heart was broken. She had believed Donald was God's will for her life. But now she prayed, "Lord, if not Donald, I believe you have someone or something better for me. I will trust you to bring it into my life." That's when she began to realize how she had been depending on other people. She'd clung first to Dick, then her sister Jay and her friend Diana, and finally to Donald. She had needed them to make her feel loved—to satisfy her emotional needs. Now she finally understood that only God could do that. With Donald gone from her life, she decided she had no choice but to trust God. She knew he'd been faithful so far, so she decided to trust him completely with her future.

Joni had a hard time imagining what the rest of her life would be like. And trusting God didn't take away all the pain and sadness she felt about Donald. In her loneliness and hurt, she turned more of her energy toward her art.

At first she had drawn for fun—then to occupy her time. But now she began to draw things that expressed her positive feelings of love and trust toward God. She soon had a collection of artwork demonstrating hope and beauty. People were attracted to her drawings of children, mountains, flowers, and animals. And Joni began to feel that her art might be connected to God's plan for her life.

One day a businessman named Neill Miller visited her dad's office and noticed one of Joni's drawings on the wall. "I really like that drawing," he told Mr. Eareckson. "Is it an original?"

"Yes, it is," Joni's dad replied. "My daughter drew it."

"She's quite an artist! It has both character and detail. She has a very original style. Her work shows great discipline."

"Thank you, I'll tell her," Mr. Eareckson said, smiling proudly. "You might be interested to know that Joni is paralyzed. She draws holding the pen in her mouth."

"That's even more remarkable!" Mr. Miller exclaimed as he stood up to examine the drawing more closely. "Absolutely amazing. Has she exhibited her artwork anywhere?"

"Just a couple of art festivals," Mr. Eareckson said. "She does it for fun. For friends and family."

"We can't let such talent go unnoticed," Mr. Miller said. "Do you think she'd mind if I arranged a small art exhibit for her?"

Joni's dad smiled and shook his head. "I'm sure she'd be delighted."

The "small" art exhibit was scheduled at a Baltimore restaurant. Jay and Diana gave Joni a ride and, when they turned the last corner, they found the street blocked off. "That's strange," Joni said. "Must be a parade. Look."

"A brass band!" Jay exclaimed. Then they all gasped because the band was standing in front of the restaurant under a huge banner, which was draped across the front of the building. It said, "Joni Eareckson Day." A television crew and a whole crowd of people were waiting for their arrival.

Joni wanted to hide. Or at least turn around and go home. But it was too late for that.

As Jay and Mr. Miller lifted her out of the car, Joni whispered, "What have you done, Mr. Miller?"

Before he could say anything, reporters surrounded Joni. Someone handed her a big bouquet, and a city hall official read a proclamation from the mayor announcing Local Art Appreciation Week and Joni Eareckson Day. Joni couldn't believe it. But she was pleased that the reporters asked more questions about her art than her wheelchair. And she was even more pleased that a lot of people liked and bought her artwork.

Later Mr. Miller told Joni, "I'm sorry if this bothered you at first. But I don't believe in doing things in a small way. And I think your sights have been set too low. You don't realize just how good your art is."

When the crowd began to thin at one point, Mr. Miller brought a tall, good-looking man over and introduced him. His hands were stuffed in his pockets, and he looked uncomfortable.

"I wanted him to talk with you, Joni," Mr. Miller said. Then he walked away, leaving the two alone and obviously feeling awkward.

The man sat down next to Joni, who tried to break the ice by asking, "What do you do?"

"Nothing," he paused. "I used to be a fireman, but I can't work anymore."

Joni didn't know what else to say. "Will you tell me about it?"

"There was an accident."

"Yes?" Joni still didn't know what his problem was.

"Well, Miller thought I should talk to you," he continued. "Miller said you had a rough time a while back . . . with your . . . handicap.

Joni nodded. "I sure did. I was so depressed that I might have killed myself if I could have used my arms."

A look of pain twisted his face. He pulled his arms out of his coat pockets. He had no hands. Just scarred stumps at the end of his arms.

He explained that he's lost his hands in a fire. "They're gone. And I just can't cope." His voice broke.

Joni told him she understood how he felt—the anger and the helplessness were natural. She talked about her experiences at the various hospitals, about learning to write and draw, about her times of discouragement, and how she'd finally learned to trust God and allowed him to work in her life.

They talked for half an hour. And when he left, the man said, "Thanks, Joni. Neill Miller was right. You have helped me. I'll try again. (That man eventually went on to rediscover an enthusiasm for life and worked as chief spokesman in the Baltimore school system for the city fire department.)

By the time the art exhibit ended, Joni had sold a thousand dollars' worth of drawings at $50 to $75 apiece. The exposure also got her invited to appear on a local TV talk show, and a major newspaper ran a big feature story.

That exhibit launched Joni's art career. She was soon receiving invitations to participate in other local art shows. She was asked to speak at churches and women's clubs, where she displayed her artwork and shared her faith in God. There was a special tour of the White House and a number of other television and radio appearances.

Joni was thrilled to be earning money and beginning to support herself. She created a line of greeting cards, started her own company, "Joni PTL," and even became a partner in a new Christian bookstore.

Then in the summer of 1974, she received an invitation to go to New York and appear on NBC's *Today* show. Barbara Walters interviewed her.

Afterward, Jay told her sister, "Just think, Joni. You probably talked to twenty or thirty million people this morning about your faith!"

Joni thought that was amazing. It hadn't been so long ago that she'd been too nervous to talk in front of fifteen kids in a small church youth group. Now here she was in New York City sharing her faith with millions of viewers on national television.

In the weeks and months that followed, Joni received more invitations to speak and appear on broadcasts than she could possibly accept. PaperMate, the company that made the Flair pens she used to draw with, set up a series of national art exhibits for her work. Her story appeared in dozens of newspapers and magazines. And a publisher called to ask if she'd like to write a book about her experiences.

Joni had a hard time believing readers would be that interested in her story. But the book *Joni* became an international best-seller. Many readers from all over the world wrote to tell her how much the book had meant to them.

So many amazing things happened after Joni decided to trust God with the rest of her life. What was most amazing was the fact that the book wasn't her big focus. She was most excited about the peace she had in her heart and the joy she sensed even when she had to go through physical setbacks. She began to wonder what else could possibly be in store for her.

10

NATIONAL RECOGNITION

World Wide Pictures bought the movie rights to her best-selling book and asked Joni to play herself. She wondered how hard it might be to relive all the difficult things that had happened to her since the accident. But Joni agreed to play the role because she thought more people might understand the message of God's love if they saw the real person instead of an actress on the screen.

The movie began with the diving scene. An actress who looked just like Joni swam out to the raft, pulled herself out of the water, and stood there for a few moments in her blue swimsuit before she dove back in.

"Cut," the director yelled. "Now we're ready for Joni."

Two paramedics loaded her on a rubber raft and floated her out into the shallow bay. They slid her into the water where she floated on her back as the rest of the cast and the cameras moved into position. At the director's signal, Joni took a deep breath and the paramedics flipped her so she was face down in the water.

Underneath the water Joni heard the call for "Action!" Then she heard the actress playing her sister Kathy come splashing into the scene and call her name. Seconds ticked by. The bay felt cold and dark. Joni was about to shake her head to signal that she needed air. But at that very moment, she felt hands lifting her out of the water, and she sputtered and gasped for breath. That didn't take a lot of acting. Then she delivered her first lines, "Kathy! I can't move. I can't feel." The cranes and cameras followed as Joni was carried to shore.

"Cut! It's a print."

Things didn't go that smoothly the day they filmed the scene where Joni's boyfriend smuggled the puppy into her hospital room. Joni wanted to get the scene over with because they had her lying face down in the Stryker Frame for a long time.

Cooper, the actor who played her boyfriend Dick, pulled the puppy out of his jacket, said his lines, and held the pup up to Joni's face. But the little dog just whined and tried to squirm free. "Cut!" the director yelled.

Four puppies and fifteen takes later, Joni gave the crew permission to smear liver-flavored baby food on the side of her face away from the camera. "Action." The puppy squirmed again, until he got a whiff of the liver and began licking Joni's face like crazy.

"Cut. That's a wrap!" All the crew cheered and applauded.

Another hospital scene required Joni and Cooper to kiss. When her boyfriend used to visit her, they never had any privacy in the ward. The visiting rooms were always full. So, to be alone, Dick would push Joni's wheelchair onto an elevator and punch the button for a lower floor. Then he'd hit "stop" between floors and they could be alone—until the nursing supervisor caught them one evening.

Joni's sister Jay teased her ahead of time about kissing a handsome Hollywood actor. And Joni was nervous about doing a kissing scene in front of so many people with someone she hardly knew. It had been so long since she'd been kissed by a boy that the night before the scene was scheduled, she practiced the best kisses she could remember—on her wrist.

There was hardly enough room in the elevator for Joni and Cooper and all the lights and camera equipment. The crew pushed Joni into the corner of the elevator, Cooper sat on her lap, and the director yelled "Action!" When the director finally yelled "Cut!" Cooper pulled away and laughed as he patted Joni's hand. "Boy, you kiss good!" he said.

"Okay, let's do that one again," the director ordered.

Once more Cooper leaned over, and he and Joni kissed a little longer than they had before. "Hey!" the director yelled. "We don't need another take, you two!" Everyone laughed.

A short time later, the crew went out to Rancho Los Amigos to shoot some of the rehab scenes. While there, Joni spotted a teenaged boy sitting rigid in a full body cast. A metal halo bolted into his head held his neck straight as it healed. She watched him painting some disks like she'd started on. "You're moving your arms, that's a good sign," she told him. Then they talked awhile as Joni answered his questions about her life and the making of the film.

Later, one of the Rancho Los Amigos staffers, Debbie Stone, told Joni more about the boy in the halo cast. "His parents won't have anything to do with him," she said.

Joni found that hard to believe. "Why?" she asked. He obviously needed his family now more than ever.

"He broke his neck in a motorcycle accident—driving while drunk," Debbie said, sadly shaking her head. "His parents figure that he got himself into this mess, so he will just have to get himself out of it."

Joni wished she had said more to the boy. She wished there was some way she could help him.

"Joni, you wouldn't believe the problems most disabled people face," Debbie said. Polio had left her confined to a wheelchair, so Joni knew she spoke from personal experience as well as from her observations working with patients in a rehab hospital. "They not only have spiritual struggles, they have a lot of down-to-earth, practical problems too."

That conversation reminded Joni how thankful she should be that she'd had so many caring and loving family members and friends to help take care of her. Not everyone in her circumstances had that.

The movie was finally finished. And, like her book, its release took her story around the world, bringing even more invitations to speak and more response from viewers who wrote to say that her story had inspired them.

But she never could forget the teenaged boy she had met or the conversation she'd had with Debbie Stone that day at Ranchos Los Amigos. And the more she thought about it, the more Joni began to think she was beginning to see what God had in mind for the next stage of her life.

★

"You sure you know what you're doing?" Jay asked as she and Joni watched their other two sisters, Kathy and Linda, carry the last of the boxes and suitcases out to the waiting pickup.

Joni smiled and nodded. She was almost thirty years old. She'd written a book and made a major motion picture about her life. But she believed there was a lot more God wanted her to do. Outside the walls of her cozy Maryland home, beyond the pastures of her family's farm, she knew there were thousands of disabled people—men and women, young people and children—who didn't have the kind of help she'd always received. They needed encouragement from God's Word, which she could share in speeches, books, and even movies. They also needed practical, everyday help from God's people. And somehow she believed God was going to help her give it—through a brand-new ministry she was starting called "Joni and Friends."

Los Angeles seemed like a good place to start. She'd made a lot of contacts out there during the making of the movie. The Billy Graham Association loaned her a woman named Judy Butler for a year to help get the ministry up and running. Judy and Joni's cousin Kerbe would live with Joni in a house provided by the staff and congregation of Grace Community Church.

Saying good-bye to her family and leaving the Maryland home she had lived in all her life was difficult. But heading west on a new adventure, entering a new stage of life, was exciting as well.

As soon as she arrived in California, Joni went to see Dr. Sam Britten at the Center for Achievement for the Physically Disabled at California State University. She wanted to talk to him about what "Joni and Friends" might do to help the disabled. But first Dr. Britten wanted to help Joni.

"Have you considered learning how to drive?" he asked her.

"The best universities in the country have tested me," she told him. "Everyone agrees that I don't have the muscles to turn a steering wheel."

"If you're open to it," Dr. Sam said, "I've got an evaluation scheduled. Right now."

After examining her and running her through some tests, he said, "Your evaluation looks great!" And he suggested some simple strengthening exercises for her shoulders and upper arms.

"Driving, huh?" Joni challenged him.

"You can do it," he told her. "I know you can. We'll worry about the steering wheel later."

Joni laughed at the idea of driving down a southern California freeway. She figured that Dr. Sam would be laughing too if he'd ever seen one of her electric wheelchair races.

11

PEOPLE PLUS

Joni stopped laughing when the congregation of Dr. Sam's church surprised her with a new cream-colored van for her ministry. He said it would help get her message to more people. Of course, she'd have to learn to drive it first. And he was serious.

A special lift raised Joni into her van. The driver's seat had been removed so she could sit right in her wheelchair. Push-button controls allowed her to start the van with a jab of a mouth stick. There was no steering wheel. Joni's hand and forearm fit into a special cuff that controlled the speed, the brakes, and even the steering.

She could hardly believe it the first time Dr. Sam took her driving on some back roads near the center. She was driving. Just like everybody else. After quite a bit more practice, Joni realized she really could drive safely, even on the freeways. Of course, she still had to convince the people at the Department of Motor Vehicles.

It did take a while to figure out how Joni could take the written test because all the desks were designed for people to take the exams standing up. Joni talked the examiner into taping a pencil to her brace and propping a wastebasket upside down on her lap to hold the test paper at the right height.

The road test was actually easier. The examiner was quite fascinated to see that Joni could drive at all. He was so amazed that he forgot to tell her where to turn and when to park. Joni passed her test with flying colors.

Joni was thrilled! She had a driver's license. That meant she could drive to meet someone for dinner. She could drive to work at Joni and Friends. She could take a drive to watch the sun set. But the best thing in Joni's mind was that she could drive alone. For the first time in the years since her accident, she could go somewhere, anywhere, by herself.

She told people, "It's almost like getting healed!"

One day Dr. Sam asked Joni if she would talk to some of his students. Everyone seemed to be listening intently except for Vicky, a beautiful young woman with dark, curly hair.

Joni was curious about this woman. She could tell Vicky was hurting; she didn't really participate like the other students at the center. Then Joni learned Vicky's story: Her husband had left her.

Forced to care for their two-year-old son alone, she had gone looking for a job. But a man who had offered her a job attacked her and then shot her in the neck, leaving her paralyzed. Three years had passed and Vicky felt she had tried everything. She had even gone to a special treatment center in Russia, hoping they could help her walk again. But she was still paralyzed. Now she was living on her own with only a part-time paid attendant and her five-year-old son to take care of her.

The more Joni watched and learned about Vicky, the more she felt God wanted her to try to help this woman and be her friend. So she asked Vicky to have dinner with her. Everything was fine when they talked about Vicky's son Arturo. Vicky even talked a little about herself. But as soon as Joni mentioned God, Vicky said it was time for her to go home.

When Joni asked her friend Rana what she had done wrong in Vicky's case, Rana told her, "I don't know how to put this. But you can't just waltz into someone's life and act like you have an easy answer for all their problems. Because you don't."

Joni realized her friend was right. She prayed that she hadn't blown her chance—that God would help her find another way to befriend Vicky. Then one day, she read Matthew 25 and saw the verse where Jesus said, "I was thirsty and you gave me something to drink. . . . I tell you the truth, whatever you did for one of the least of these brothers of mine, you did for me."

That's when it hit. She wasn't just supposed to talk and give advice. She needed to begin by doing small, practical things to help meet people's needs—to do these things as if she were doing them for Jesus himself.

The first thing Joni did was offer Vicky one of her corsets. "It helps me breathe and sit up straight," she explained. "It's the only reason I can sing or even talk loudly."

Vicky agreed to try it, so Rana and Joni's friend and assistant Judy lifted Vicky onto a bed, rolled her to get the corset under her, and then fastened it in place. Back in her wheelchair, Vicky said, "Oh, my goodness! What a difference this makes in my voice!"

Joni shared some other practical tips with Vicky and even offered to loan her an extra easel so she could begin to learn to write with a pen in her mouth. "Maybe we could show your attendant how to . . ."

"My last attendant left," Vicky said with a sigh. "Thank goodness."

"Why do you say that?" Joni wanted to know. She had never been without family and friends to help take care of her.

"We got in this argument," Vicky admitted. "She got so angry that she took a pillow and put it over . . ." she paused and her eyes filled with tears.

" . . . over my face. She wanted to kill me. Luckily my brother was upstairs at the time. When he heard me scream, he came running, grabbed my attendant by the hair, threw her out the door, and told her never to come back.

"Now all I have is Arturo. But he's just a little boy. He and I can't go on like this. I need someone."

"Let's start by praying," Rana suggested.

Vicky's angry response startled Joni and her friends. "Jesus can't help me! Jesus can't put me to bed or get me up in the morning! He can't get me a drink of water," she said. "It's nice for you that you believe in God. But I need somebody more—more real than God. I need people."

Joni knew she had to choose her words carefully. "I need people too," she told Vicky. "But I know that Kerbe and Judy and Rana and others are like . . . like the hands of God for me. It is Jesus who gets me up in the morning. He just uses people to do the work that needs to be done."

"Have any of your people ever tried to murder you?" Vicky asked.

Joni didn't know how to answer.

But a few days later, Joni and Rana and Judy went out to dinner to discuss how they might help Vicky. "What has helped you the most, Joni?" Judy wanted to know.

"My situation has been so different," Joni said. "My family is unusually close. And I've got great friends. Like Vicky said, it's people who really make the difference."

"Well," Judy said and grinned.

"Well what?" Joni wasn't sure what her friend was getting at. "Do I stick you two in a copy machine and pass out copies?" She wished she could. So many people like Vicky needed help.

"Sort of," Judy replied. "Why don't you train people—teach them to help like we do?"

"Do you mean we should offer a class?" Joni asked. "We should teach people how to push a wheelchair, lift a person in and out of bed, or whatever?"

"Maybe they'll even learn to empty a leg bag," Rana added. "Christians are supposed to be servants and care about people in need, right?"

Joni and her friends got so excited that they started writing ideas and plans down on the back of their napkins. Over a hundred people—college students, mothers, teachers, nurses, businessmen—came to their first "People Plus" workshop. That was the beginning of the volunteer training, family camps, Bible studies, daily radio broadcasts, and all the other outreach programs that Joni and Friends is involved in today.

It wasn't long until Vicky was one of those friends—trusting God herself and helping Joni show his love by helping to meet the needs of the disabled—one person at a time.

12

JONI AND KEN

One Friday night Joni watched her cousin hurrying around the apartment preparing for a date. Ready to go at last, Kerbe pulled a spray bottle out of her purse. "Want some perfume?" she asked.

"I'm not going anywhere," Joni told her.

"That's not the point." She squirted a little scent on Joni's neck anyway.

After Kerbe left, the lingering smell of perfume took Joni back in her memory to the days when she had regular Friday night dates. She chuckled to herself. Guys weren't exactly beating down the door to take her out now.

The following Sunday morning, a guest speaker in church preached a longer than usual sermon. Joni tried to concentrate. But her mind wandered. Her eyes roamed until she noticed a man with a thick, dark head of hair sitting a few rows ahead of her. Since she couldn't seem to take her eyes off the man, she felt the urge to pray for him. And that's what she did for the rest of the sermon.

After the service, Joni thought about introducing herself to the man and telling him what she'd been doing. But she thought, *He'll just think I'm crazy*. So she put him out of her mind.

But a month or so later, a friend at church introduced Joni to a nice-looking man with Asian features. Joni thought he looked vaguely familiar. Then it hit her. "Turn around," she told him. "I want to see the back of your head."

He gave her a funny sort of grin, but he did as she asked. Sure enough, he was the man with the thick black hair. "I prayed for the back of your head a few weeks ago," Joni told him. They both laughed, and she went on to explain what had happened.

They chatted for a few moments and said good-bye. But as she turned and powered her wheelchair toward the exit, Joni realized she's already forgotten the man's name. She whirled the chair around and asked him again.

"Ken Tada." He smiled and waved good-bye.

To her surprise, Joni kept running into Ken Tada. At church. At a Young Life meeting. Finally, a couple of her church friends decided to try a little matchmaking and invited Ken to Joni's birthday party.

Off and on during the evening, Joni noticed Ken. She noticed that he seemed to be comfortable talking to people, and he had an easy smile. When he walked over at the end of the party to say good night, he leaned against the wall beside Joni's chair, and they chatted a few minutes. She learned he taught high school social studies and coached football.

Finally Joni said she had to leave—she had a long drive home. Ken said, "I'd like to continue this conversation. How about over dinner next Friday?"

"I'd like that," Joni told him.

A florist delivered a bouquet of roses to her house the next morning. Kerbe opened the card and read Joni the note: "Looking forward to Friday. Ken Tada."

On Friday, Ken arrived dressed in a nice blue suit—with more flowers. Judy and Kerbe gave him a crash course in how to lift Joni, how to straighten her in the wheelchair, how to tuck her jacket in the back so it wouldn't wrinkle, and how to pull down the inseam of her slacks. He seemed to pay close attention to the details.

Then he wheeled Joni out to his car, took off his jacket, and rolled up his sleeves. He squatted beside Joni's chair to lift her. With a mighty karate "hi-ya!" he heaved her to his chest and carefully set her back down in the front seat. Judy showed him how to fold the chair and stow it in the trunk.

"You really aren't heavy at all," he said, backing out of the driveway. "Light as a feather, in fact."

"Oh, really?" Joni thought she'd tease him a bit. "Based on that weight-lifting move back there, I never would have known."

"Well, I have been working out—lifting weights," he replied.

"How much weight did you train with?" Joni asked.

"Oh, about one hundred and seventy-five pounds."

"A hundred and what?" Joni exclaimed.

"I wanted to make sure I didn't drop you." Then he grinned, and Joni realized he was teasing her.

"Just so you don't think I weigh a hundred and seventy-five," Joni told him.

"Oh, don't worry," he said with a mischievous grin. "I could tell how much you really weigh."

When they got to the restaurant where Ken had made reservations, there was no wheelchair ramp. No problem. "I can handle those stairs," he told Joni. He wheeled her to the bottom step, turned her around, tilted her back, and pulled her up one step at time. "Easy," he said.

Joni was impressed with how comfortable he seemed. Handling her chair. Cutting her shrimp. Giving her a bite of his appetizer and holding her glass so she could drink her water. That made *her* feel comfortable too.

"You've been around disabled people, haven't you?" she asked as she scooped up another bite of shrimp.

"Yes and no," Ken replied. And he told her about volunteering with the Special Olympics. "But dating someone in a wheelchair—no. I've never done that."

"Well," Joni grinned. "There's something else you're gonna have to do that you've never done before."

"What's that?" Ken asked.

"My leg bag needs emptying," Joni told him.

"Okay," he said. "Just tell me what to do."

He paid the check and pushed Joni toward the restrooms. But he stopped suddenly in the hallway. He stared first at the Ladies' room and then at the Men's. "Uh, I think we have a problem here," he said.

"Well," Joni teased, "I hadn't thought about this one."

People were walking around them, going in and out of the restroom doors. "Come on, Joni," Ken whispered. "What should I do?"

"I think maybe we should head outside and find a tree," she told him.

"A tree?"

Joni grinned. "Well, I think that would be a lot classier than a fire hydrant, don't you?"

★

Joni and Ken spent a lot of time together over the next few months. One night, sitting on her sofa in front of the fireplace, he told her, "Joni, I tell you things about myself that I don't tell just anybody. And I feel strong, not just emotionally but spiritually, when I'm with you. But ..." He paused before he went on. "It's like this. When the kids I teach come to me and want advice about dating, especially when they're upset because they've just broken up with someone, you know what I tell them? I let them know that when they decide to date somebody seriously, it's going to end up one of two ways. Either they will marry that person, or they will break up and never really be close again."

"So," Joni said, "you're afraid if we keep spending time together ... as friends ... or whatever ..."

"That's just it, Joni," Ken said. "It's awfully hard for two people ... a man and a woman in their thirties, single ... it's hard to be just friends. I want it that way, really—but then again, I don't. So I guess I'm gonna have to swallow the same advice I give those high school kids ...." his voice drifted off.

He leaned closer to Joni, "I can't imagine not being close to you." Then he put his hand around the back of her neck and kissed her.

"I'm afraid," Joni whispered.

"I know," Ken told her. "So am I."

As time went by, Ken and Joni grew even closer. They went everywhere together. Ken even took

Joni to Disneyland. "What do you want to try first?" he asked.

"Let's try that new wild roller coaster on the other side of the park," Joni told him. "I think we can handle it."

Ken plopped his Mickey Mouse ears on her head and wedged a box of popcorn between Joni's knees. "Let's go then. The lines will probably be a mile long."

"Ah, but I have a secret." Joni smiled.

He followed behind Joni's chair as she wheeled around the lines outside the attraction. "We can't just cut to the front," he said.

"I'm not cutting in front," Joni told him. "I'm cutting in back. Come on." When they got to the exit, an attendant opened the door and motioned them right inside. "See?" She grinned.

Ken and the attendant lifted her right into a waiting bobsled. The boy buckled her in while Ken slid in behind her. The car behind them slammed into the back of their sled.

"I'm not ready!" Joni yelled. "Am I in?"

"You're in," Ken told her. "Here we go."

"Hold me," Joni called out. "I don't have any balance."

The trouble was that Ken had to let go of his handholds to hold Joni. So both of their bodies slammed from one side of the sled to the other at every turn. Ken giggled hysterically and Joni screamed, "I think I'm going to die!"

When they finally reached the end of the ride, the attendant laughed to see them both lying flat on the bottom of the sled. "We let disabled people ride twice if they want," he said. "Saves them the hassle of getting in and out again."

"You're kidding," Joni said. "You must be trying to get rid of us."

"Let's do it, Joni." Ken laughed as he scooted up behind her and the car behind jolted them forward once more.

"What? No, not again," Joni said.

"Too late!" Ken yelled, laughing and wrapping his arms around her. The sled took off for a second run.

Afterward, as they went out the exit, Ken was still laughing. Smiling, Joni flung her arm out to hit him. "I could have been killed," she said. Then she started laughing too.

Later, at dinner, Ken said, "Being disabled has its advantages. No standing in lines at Disneyland. Going in exits. Riding twice. Even the parking places are bigger." He took her hand. "Knowing you is a real plus, Joni—in more ways that one."

Knowing Ken proved to be a big plus for Joni as well. Two years later, they were married. Joni Eareckson Tada began a whole new chapter in her life with someone who promised that they would try to do God's will—together.

13

A GLOBAL MINISTRY

More than three decades have passed since her diving accident in Chesapeake Bay. Yet today, Joni Eareckson Tada seems to have more energy than when she was a teenager. She and Ken have now been married almost twenty years. And the Tadas lead very busy lives.

In the 1980s, Presidents Reagan and Bush appointed Joni to the National Council on Disability. She served on that council and was a leading advocate in helping the Americans with Disabilities Act become law. Through her ongoing work with Joni and Friends, she records a five-minute radio program heard daily on more than 850 stations. She is a popular conference speaker, both in the United States and internationally. She's authored almost thirty books and received countless awards and honors for her ministry to the disabled.

Joni and Ken both serve on the board of Joni and Friends (JAF), which, since its beginning in 1979, has been dedicated to sharing the love and message of Christ in practical ways with people affected by disabilities—whether it is the disabled person, a family member, or a friend.

JAF also is committed to recruiting, training, and motivating a new generation of people with disabilities to become leaders in their churches and communities. In addition, JAF seeks to equip and mobilize churches to minister to the disabled. The team does this by providing churches with effective programs, training, and materials. From local neighborhoods to the far reaches of the world, Joni and Friends is striving to demonstrate to disabled people that God has not abandoned them.

Everywhere she goes, Joni challenges churches and individuals to take part in Christian outreach to the disabled in communities around the globe. She constantly reminds people of Jesus' instruction in Luke 14:13, 23, which says, "But when you give a banquet, invite the poor, the crippled, the lame, the blind and you will be blessed . . . . Make them come in, so that my house will be full."

For a long time after her accident, Joni wondered how God could ever bring anything good out of her suffering and circumstances. After many years, she slowly understood God's plan and purposes. Mainly,

God wanted to give her his joy and peace and he could only do that as Joni would learn to lean hard on him. This is why Joni is able to accept her wheelchair. It helps her go to God for help each and every day. It's also the message behind the *Joni* book. She wants other people to learn to see their suffering as something that can draw them closer to Jesus.

And now, thirty-five years later, millions of people around the world have heard or seen her story. The book *Joni* has been translated into forty-five languages and sold millions of copies. Thousands have been drawn to Christ because of her message of hope.

Consider the story of Dr. Zhang Xu, an orthopedic surgeon who lives in Anshan, northeast of Beijing, in China. Dr. Zhang was working in the Middle East when he dove into shallow water and broke his neck. He suffered many complications, and by the time he was sent home to China, he was near death.

A Japanese therapist who helped Xu gave him a tattered copy of *Joni* in English. Dr. Zhang Xu slowly read the account of another person who had been injured in much the same way. She, too, had been asked to lay aside her shattered dreams and find new meaning for her life. He was deeply encouraged to know that he was not alone in his heartbreaking journey. Someone else understood. More importantly, God understood.

Immediately Dr. Zhang began translating Joni's book into simplified Chinese text. Late into the night, with the book propped on a stand, Xu translated each word to his mother who, by the glow of a desk lamp, wrote down every word in pencil. Xu and his mother wanted very much to share the story of Joni with thousands of disabled people in their vast nation. It took them many months, but when they finally finished, they had a manuscript a foot and a half high!

Two years later, Joni and Ken attended a press conference at the China Rehabilitation Research Center in Beijing, where Dr. Zhang and Joni were guests of honor. The book had just been published in Chinese, and Joni was there to hand out hundreds of hot-off-the-press copies to disabled people and their families at the center. And that was just the beginning. Because the *Joni* book has helped open doors, JAF has been allowed to distribute wheelchairs in China and work with churches to reach out with more help for people with disabilities.

Stories like this one have happened not only in China but all over the world. And things are still happening in the United States as well.

We'll close with a story Joni tells in her own words:

"My heart was warmed when I received this note: 'My mother bought me your first book in 1983 after

I broke my neck in an auto accident. My husband, Larry, would lie on the floor under my Stryker Frame and hold the book up so I could read it. You are such a motivation to people like me with disabilities. Keep it up! Love, Lenda.'

"I looked up from Lenda's note and recalled what it felt like, nearly three and a half decades ago, to lie face down on a Stryker Frame. The restraining straps, the stiffness in my neck, staring at the floor tiles and fighting off claustrophobia. I recall how my father fashioned a little stool just high enough to fit underneath my Stryker Frame. He would place a book on it so I could reach the pages with my mouth stick. One of the first books I asked for was the Bible (I tried very hard not to drool on it!).

"Why the Bible? I had a zillion questions, and I was desperate for answers. You now know the rest of the story. Yes, I found some helpful answers, but more importantly, I found the One who holds all the answers in his hand.

"This is why I wrote the book *Joni*. I knew there would be thousands of people, like me, who would follow in my 'wheelchair tracks.' They too would have heart-wrenching questions. They also would lie in hospital beds and wonder about the future. I also knew there would be thousands more who would not experience a broken neck, but a broken heart or broken home.

"When I wrote *Joni* in 1976, I believed the book would have universal appeal. And in the new millennium, it continues to speak volumes to those who hurt.

"I'm in my fifties now and, with it, I am facing a whole new set of aches and pains, limitations and challenges. But rather than worry about the future, I'll remember Lenda's words: 'Keep it up!' I'll keep trusting God one day at a time. I will say 'yes' to the offer of his strength and power and 'no' to grumbling, no matter if I face a four-week stint in bed with pressure sores, or a flat tire on my wheelchair when I'm cruising the Thousand Oaks mall.

"I will keep being a supportive wife to my husband of nearly twenty years, Ken Tada. Through Joni and Friends, we will continue to spread God's good news around the world to people with disabilities and their families. We will keep traveling to our JAF Family Retreats, connecting with scores of moms and dads and disabled children. We will keep ministering through Wheels for the World, our program through which we take refurbished wheelchairs to needy disabled people overseas, as well as Bibles and disability ministry training materials for churches. We will keep advocating for families affected by disability to improve the quality of life and care, whether here in the U.S. or around the world.

"I will keep on keeping on, by the grace of God. As long as I can sit up in this chair and as long as my lungs hold out, I will echo Isaiah 12:5

and 'Sing to the LORD, for he has done glorious things; let this be known to all the world.'

"Come to think of it, even if I can't sit up in my chair, I'll keep on keeping on. Lying on my back, I'll be forced to look up—into the heart of heaven, into the face of my Lord Jesus.

"And by the grace of God . . . I'll keep smiling."

Joni has formed an organization called **JONI AND FRIENDS** to encourage Christian ministry to the disabled.

If your mom or dad (or any other adult member of your family) would like to learn more about **JONI AND FRIENDS**, as well as receive information regarding her books, tapes, videos, and cassettes (many are for children), please have them write to:

JONI AND FRIENDS
Department Z
P.O. Box 3333
Agoura Hills, CA 91301

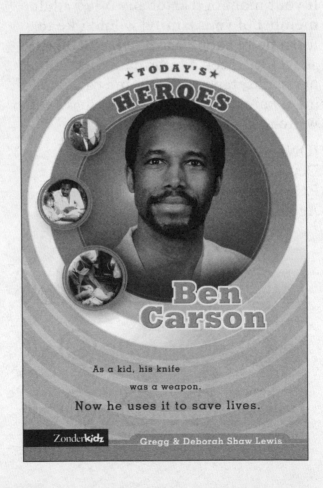

1

THE DUMBEST KID IN FIFTH GRADE

Hey, Dummy!"

Ben Carson looked up. "Dummy" was the nickname his classmates had given him.

Another fifth grader laughed at Ben's instinctive response: "Ben Carson is *so* dumb."

Ben shrugged and tried to act as if he didn't mind. He didn't like being called dumb. Who would? But he figured what the kid said was true. After all, he heard it every single day.

"Ben Carson's the dumbest kid in fifth grade!" the kid continued.

Ben looked the other way. He wasn't in the mood to argue.

"Hey, Carson's the dumbest kid in the world!" someone else called out.

Now wait a minute! Ben thought. *I know I'm dumb. I have plenty of test grades to prove that. But surely somewhere in the world there has to be someone dumber than I am!*

It was time to draw the line. "I'm *not* the dumbest kid in the world!"

"You are too!"

"I am not!" Ben insisted.

"Couldn't be anybody in the world dumber than you are, Carson!"

The two argued back and forth until the teacher called the class inside.

Later that same afternoon, there was a math quiz. Afterward, the teacher had each student pass his test to the person behind him to correct as the teacher read out the answers. Ben knew what was coming next. Each student would have to report his or her score to the teacher—out loud!

Ben stared with disgust at the big fat zero on the top of his paper. *This oughta be good*, he thought. *When everybody finds out what I made on this quiz, they'll never let up.*

That's when Ben began to scheme: *Maybe if I mumble*, he thought, *the teacher won't understand me.* So when the teacher called his name, he muttered, "Nnme." And it worked!

"Nine! Benjamin? How wonderful! Class, can you see what Benjamin has done? Didn't I tell you if you just applied yourself you could do it? I'm so proud of you!"

We want to hear from you. Please send your comments about this
book to us in care of the address below. Thank you.

Grand Rapids, MI 49530
www.zonderkidz.com